Dear Parent:
Your child's love of reading starts here!

Every child learns to read in a different way and at his or her own speed. Some go back and forth between reading levels and read favorite books again and again. Others read through each level in order. You can help your young reader improve and become more confident by encouraging his or her own interests and abilities. From books your child reads with you to the first books he or she reads alone, there are I Can Read Books for every stage of reading:

SHARED READING
Basic language, word repetition, and whimsical illustrations, ideal for sharing with your emergent reader

BEGINNING READING
Short sentences, familiar words, and simple concepts for children eager to read on their own

READING WITH HELP
Engaging stories, longer sentences, and language play for developing readers

READING ALONE
Complex plots, challenging vocabulary, and high-interest topics for the independent reader

I Can Read Books have introduced children to the joy of reading since 1957. Featuring award-winning authors and illustrators and a fabulous cast of beloved characters, I Can Read Books set the standard for beginning readers.

A lifetime of discovery begins with the magical words "I Can Read!"

Visit www.icanread.com for information
on enriching your child's reading experience.

For my sobrinita Charli,
style as bright as the city
¡te quiero!
—E.O.

To Alex, Jeremy, and all the beautiful
friends from abroad who have
opened their arms and hearts.
—A.L.

I Can Read® and I Can Read Book® are trademarks of HarperCollins Publishers.

Reina Ramos: Tour Guide
Text copyright © 2024 by Emma Otheguy
Illustrations copyright © by Andrés Landazábal
All rights reserved. Manufactured in Malaysia.
No part of this book may be used or reproduced in any manner whatsoever without written permission except
in the case of brief quotations embodied in critical articles and reviews. For information address
HarperCollins Children's Books, a division of HarperCollins Publishers,
195 Broadway, New York, NY 10007.
www.icanread.com

Library of Congress Control Number: 2023936870
ISBN 978-0-06-322322-6 (trade bdg.) — ISBN 978-0-06-322319-6 (pbk.)

Book design by Elaine Lopez
23 24 25 26 27 COS 10 9 8 7 6 5 4 3 2 1   First Edition

Reina Ramos

Tour Guide

by Emma Otheguy
pictures by Andrés Landazábal

HARPER
An Imprint of HarperCollinsPublishers

My cousin Andrés is visiting!

We meet him at the airport.

I hold a banner that says

¡BIENVENIDO!

Abuela shouts his name.

Everybody hugs.

On the bus home,

I look at Andrés.

He is two years older

and a whole lot taller than me.

I have not seen him in a long time!

I wonder if we will have fun.

Mami unfolds the couch
for Andrés to sleep on.

Abuela puts on our favorite song—
it's by Celia Cruz!
Everyone dances.

While we have lunch,
Abuela and Andrés have LOTS to say.
Andrés has all the latest news
from the island—
but I've never been!

Abuela asks tons of questions
about family I've never met.

After lunch, we scooter to the park.

My friends are excited

to meet Andrés.

Carlos has been to the island.

"I love the palm trees," Carlos says.

"Sí," Andrés says,

"and the food is so good."

They close their eyes

and imagine the yummy food.

At bedtime, I ask Mami,

"Can we go to the island?"

"Maybe someday," she says.

"Right now it's hard to travel."

I frown.

This is really unfair!

Mami tucks me in.

"Enjoy your primo.

We're lucky he is here."

But I'm not feeling lucky.

I just feel left out.

Andrés is still talking

about the island the next morning.

I go to Mami's room.

"I wish he would stop," I say.

"Maybe Andrés talks about home because he is homesick," Mami says.

"Homesick?" I say.

"He's having a great time!"

"You can be both," Mami says.

After breakfast,

we take Andrés sightseeing.

We go to the subway stop.

When we get on the train,

Andrés stands next to Abuela.

He is still talking about the island!

SCREECH!

The subway stops suddenly.

Andrés slams into me.

He knocks off my crown headband!

I shout, "Andrés, stop talking

and watch out!"

"Reina!" Mami says.

She does not look happy.

I cross my arms.

"It's true.

He slammed into me!"

"¡Lo siento!" Andrés says.

"I've never ridden a subway before."

He picks up my headband.

"Never?" I say.

I ride the subway all the time!

"Nunca—never," Andrés says.

"Wow—your town is really different
from here," I say.

"I'm having fun visiting," Andrés says,
"but it's a little overwhelming.
Sometimes I miss home."

"I bet everyone at home
misses you too," I say.
I sigh.
"I wish I could see the island.
I've never even been!
It's like you and Abuela
are in a club without me!"

Andrés smiles.

"But you're our family!
Abuela talks about you
every time she calls."

"My mami has a photo of you
right on her dresser," Andrés says.
That makes me happy!
I love that there's a photo of me
on the island with palm trees
and yummy food.

I have an idea.

"I'll teach you about the subway.

You keep talking about the island."

I show Andrés how to hold the pole

and stay still when the subway stops.

When we bump each other, we laugh.

Andrés tells me about our family.

Abuela adds stories about them too.

It's like I'm really meeting them!

When we get off at our stop,

A musician is singing Celia Cruz songs!

She's our favorite!

Everyone grabs hands.

We all dance together!

Glossary

¡Bienvenido!: Welcome!

¡Lo siento!: I'm sorry!

Nunca: Never

Primo: Cousin

Sí: Yes